WELCOME

the first new penny dreadful for over a century to hit the streets of London. As with those Victorian magazines there are shocking serial stories on salacious subjects and some tasty illustrations to accompany them. There are differences though. In the first place it doesn't cost a penny and in the second the tales in One Eye Grey are based on folklore or ghost stories. These are recast for the modern age making for something chilling and pocket-sized to carry around with you in the heat of the summer.

A goose in Southwark brings together a fresh set of urbanites and a whole range of spooky stories as well as revealing why Carl, narrator of parts one and three, really decided to leave the city and his friends. Part three follows Carl out of the orbital to the satellite coastal towns where he learns that leaving the metropolis does not cause it to desert him. This volume is strictly a London something ranging from Southwark to the City, Bloomsbury and Holborn to Chelsea and Notting Hill, all with their own contributions to this collection of stories from another London.

Key themes within One Eye Grey are the perception people have of London, the city's shifting nature and the disappearances that happen within it. With these in mind it seems appropriate to dedicate this issue jointly to the Café Grove, formerly of Portobello Road, which closed its doors forever at the end of 2006, and also to Star Video, late of the Walworth Road. Great places which were credits to a couple of central London communities that have already suffered much from stereotyping at the hands of the British film industry and the homogenisation of our high streets.

A GOOSE IN SOUTHWARK

Some Americans have a strange view of London. They think the city is regularly enveloped in a great fog, we call each other 'guvnor' and can all quote entire episodes of Monty Python. The first two of these misapprehensions can be blamed on Sherlock Holmes films, especially for fostering the notion that London particulars are not at all peculiar, so that we spend half the winter under conditions of very poor visibility. Their view of the Brits overall seems similarly misty and whereas British humour plays well with certain sections of the US public, it doesn't do to be overly clever. At least, that was how it appeared to Shane Satey at the end of a walking tour along London's newly booming Bankside, entitled *And If You Know Your History*. The guide had so clearly flagged up imminent jokes he might as well have got out a red rag and started walking slowly before the approach of the punch line.

The odd joke, occasional ghost story and lots of history were the staple of walking tours and, Shane decided, a lengthy past was one thing Britain had over America, any way you broke it down. He thought the guides formed a strange subsection of the entertainment industry being part actor, part public speaker, part teacher and part pub raconteur.

From the other side of the bar, Shane could still hear the tour guide's voice, an annoying Scouse manqué, droning on about the river and how people once crossed it by riverboat. He was telling a yarn, almost certainly apocryphal, about a bear that had escaped from one of the amphitheatres mid-baiting session, and made it to the river. The dozy ferryman assumed the creature lumbering into his boat was just a drunken fat bloke in a fur coat. The sculler was halfway across the river, and midway through a rant about all those bloody Huguenots coming in and changing the East End, before he realised his predicament and made a jump for it. It was clear from the laughter wafting across the bar that the guide still had a willing audience. Shane assumed this was because people wanted value for money and, cynically, that the guide was probably trying to cop off with the short, intense American blonde.

His account of the evening would be hostile, Shane had already decided that. It was just a question of how hostile and how to phrase it. Part of his antagonism was due to his having been given this assignment in the first place. When the Standard suggested a series of reviews on London's tourist features, he had hoped for a more interesting subject. Shane was further irked because he needed the money, and it really vexed him to watch the guide trouser more than £100 for his couple of hours' 'work', then not even have to pay for his own drinks. Shane took out his notebook and started jotting down ideas for the review. He was keen to get a pun on the word 'surbator' (meaning one who tires through walking) into the piece. He knew that if he described the guide as a 'master surbator' it would be edited out, so he started gently.

'Walking tours are a quaintly anachronistic way of passing the time, which is perhaps appropriate given that they deal largely in archaic facts. Leading swag-bellied mobs of clueless tourists through certain sections of London...'

He paused and wrote a note to himself to check out the complaints made by a number of Spitalfields residents about the Ripper tours of their area. Fair enough, he thought. After all, a tour of the Portman Road area of Ipswich or Lumb Lane Bradford, say, would hardly be deemed appropriate. Picking up his theme again, he ruminated.

'These rabbles prefer to be spoon–fed their history from a clichéd, oft–repeated script delivered, if tonight is anything to go by, by a passionless fop whose mind is clearly elsewhere. Rather than reading history books, downloading the appropriate information and exploring the areas themselves, they return voluntarily to the days of the school trip. Like those supervised visits, stragglers are encouraged to keep up and participants discouraged from exploring interesting features autonomously for the good of the assembly as a whole. This evening's event, run by the ridiculously named Foot and Mouth Walking Tour Company, took in much of the recently rejuvenated area around London Bridge and Bankside.'

Was that a little harsh, he wondered, as he took a swig from his pint. Best put in some facts from the tour itself.

'Most Londoners would probably already know the bare bones of the tour: a medley of Shakespeare, Chaucer, Pepys and, for the salacious, prostitution. But I would question why even the most bored adult tourist would want to know precisely where on Stoney Street parts of Harry Potter were filmed.

'This is the question at the heart of walking tours as a form of entertainment: exactly who are they for and what do people get from them? If all a tourist wants is safe passage through London's streets, they might be better off hiring a security guard. If they're afraid of getting lost, perhaps they should consider bringing their map-reading skills up to speed before embarking on transcontinental travel. As to locals who might be considering a walking tour, all this reviewer can say is that this is not the tour for them. Maybe there are more specialised tours that could appeal to residents. But as a general point, I'd say just walk on by.'

Shane liked that ending – he enjoyed puns on songs. He wasn't so pleased with the build up, though, he would have to work on that. He was also happy with his dig at the crowd, whose upbeat enjoyment of their evening offended his sense of cynical detachment. He might have forgiven it, however, had anyone taken more interest in him. He watched the pub begin to empty. Only a few stragglers from the party were left, including the chestnut-haired girl with the Osmonds teeth but great body. Swallowing the last of his third pint of the evening, Shane shifted towards the door, gathering his clothes about him because it was freezing outside.

It was also foggy – the Americans had got their wish on that. A proper pea-souper swirled along the banks of the Thames, virtually obscuring the hulking railway bridge opposite the pub. On the other side of the street, the new restaurants in the railway arches beckoned and the sound of a boat's horn came off the water as Shane stole away in the direction of the wine museum. He didn't see the girl slip out of the fog towards him.

'Hello, dearie. Want some company?' She was heavily wrapped up in what could have been a shawl but was just as likely a blanket. Shane decided that it was a shawl – blanket wearers usually proffered a copy of The Big Issue, not company. The girl was very pale and short, with dark hair hanging down rather lankly, and she gave off a faint smell of lavender.

The whole scene felt very strange. True, this sort of thing was not uncommon around Brick Lane, but it wasn't what one expected on Bankside. Not any more, anyway – three hundred years ago, this had been London's red light area and theatre district. That was where Maiden Lane, where Shane was now standing, had got its name from. As well as the painted doxies, there had been gambling, bear baiting and theatricals to lure people south. Shane held strong views about south London and its desirability at the best of times, and Bankside's resurrection as London's leisure district since the 1990s had been as startling to him as its new attraction as a place to live. Still, it was going too far to believe that the baggage trade had come back as well.

Shane was puzzled and a little excited. He wondered if he could get the girl into his piece somehow, and considered the possibility that it was some odd bit of performance art. He'd read about things like that but decided that it was too late and too cold and, as a well-informed young metropolitan he would surely have heard about such an event. The girl interrupted his thoughts.

'C'mon, I'm perishing cold, you'll be my last of the night. No one about in this fog.'

'What – here? Bit public, isn't it?' Shane glanced about him and realised that, actually, there was very little chance of anyone seeing anything in the current murk.

She smiled. 'I've got a spot, no one will see us. Just up here.'

She led him some way up Park Street and then across the main road under the railway bridge.

'Been to an entertainment tonight dear?' the girl asked.

Shane hadn't been expecting small talk but managed to laugh and said, 'Well, that's one way of describing it. Lot of old stories, really.'

'Not one of Mr. Shakespeare's, then? I like the romances myself, can't be doing with all that political stuff.'

Once over Southwark Street, she pulled him gently but insistently through a gap in some hoardings. On the other side Shane could see nothing, but he sensed he might be in a car park as he could feel concrete beneath his feet. The girl led him to a rough lean-to as a train thundered overhead, heading towards Cannon Street.

'In here. Don't be shy, no one can see us. Ah that's nice ain't it?' A hand ran up his jeans. 'But money first, eh?'

He handed over a twenty and tried to relax, but his heart was pounding from the rapidity of it all and a sudden fear about the location, alongside his arousal. This could easily turn out to be a mugging. The girl looked slight, but she could have confederates. Her hands began to press into his trousers and he forgot this for a few moments.

'Been drinking have you, dearie?' she asked, after nothing much happened for him except a soft spasm that told him the game was over. Feeling bewildered, though lighter, he bundled himself through the fence, muttering whatever came into his head. He even asked if he could see her again.

'Oh I'm always around here, dearie. But if you need a reminder, take this.'

He stuffed what felt like a strip of fabric into his pocket and walked along Red Cross Way. Opposite a closed pub, the Boot and Flogger, a gate led into the yard he'd just left and he noticed that the entrance was covered with ribbons and other totems. He ran the remainder of the street. From the end of it, he could see Borough High Street and a red bus flashing by in the fog. He tore towards the bus stop and caught a northbound 35. That would drop him by Echopraxia in Shoreditch where, over a few drinks, he could polish his review and mentally rewrite his account of the last part of his evening. Reaching for his Oyster, he pulled out a small ribbon, on which was written in felt tip the name Alice Street and what looked like a weird mobile number: 1678 08 06 1703.

NIGHT BUS TO ECHO

ON WEEKNIGHTS AT SUCH AN HOUR, MOST PEOPLE ARE HEADING away from the City, so the bus north was empty enough for Shane to get a front seat upstairs, which ordinarily afforded the best views across the river. Tonight the fog was too thick for that. Lights on the bridges showed their position, just, and the fog even deadened the City's customary sounds. Wisps of fog entered through the top deck windows. Shane felt as if all his senses had been altered.

In this sensory shift, Shane was beginning to wonder if his own imagination hadn't conjured up the girl. She had appeared real enough and he still had the cloth in his pocket, but the whole experience had left him bewildered. Every now and then, figures slipped through the fog, causing him to focus more sharply on them than he might normally have done, but there was only the briefest moment of clarity before they again dissolved into the murk. One of these spectres occasionally got on his bus and joined the watchers from the deck.

It was a Londoner who first coined the term 'smog' in 1905, to describe the city's then insidious combination of natural fog and coal smoke. Although tonight's smog was coating everything, it was less likely to leave lasting grime on the buildings. The older buildings were in any case uniquely suited for this weather, blending greys and shades of brown, yellow and off-white in a perfect camouflage. Shane thought of a line from Macbeth: 'Fair is foul, and foul is fair/Hover through the fog and filthy air', as he looked down from the top deck. His thoughts turned to his old English teacher, Mrs Hibbs. Room at the top indeed – here he was, cutting through the old city along the streets trodden by her heroes, Chaucer, Blake and Shakespeare.

The bus rocked onto Gracechurch Street and Shane found himself thinking about how he could make some decent money. It was too late to retrain as a broker, he supposed. Besides, he lacked the temperament for it. As they travelled up Bishopsgate, which had once been the border of old London, he thought of the passing of time, ambition and power, and realised that London fog had seen millions of his sort travelling through it. As recently as 1952, a four-day particular had killed 4,000 Londoners. Most of the people who died did so from respiratory illnesses, but a significant number lost their lives falling off bridges or into unseen traffic. Things were so bad that the blind led the sighted through the streets. Tonight, the fog was reclaiming its territory as the bus eased past Liverpool Street and veered to the left, at the beginning of a loop that would drop Shane near his destination and prime the bus for its journey back over London Bridge.

Alighting, Shane caught sight of his reflection. Dark, wavy hair, cut long but already betraying an alarming pattern around his forehead; a large nose and narrow mouth (thanks mum), from which a face Brazilian tapered to the cleft of his chin. But his jaw was ok, and he made the most of his height. He hunched his shoulders now as he walked the few minutes to Echopraxia, backtracking slightly to skirt the edge of Hoxton Square.

Echopraxia (or Eee Pee as some knew it) was not really a bar in the strict sense and certainly couldn't be described as a pub; nor was it exactly a members club. In theory, everyone who drank there was supposed to be affiliated to one of the many design studios in the converted warehouse in which it was situated, or a guest of whoever was hiring it for the night. In practice, while people affiliated to the studios did use it almost as a club, it was also a useful late-night hangout for anyone who knew of its existence and had the discretion not to talk too much about it. For this reason, a mini-drama was being played out near the entrance, involving a young couple pacing the street.

A woman, sounding annoyed, was asking where the bar was.

'You said you knew it well. You said it was easy. I missed my last tube for this!'

More in desperation than anger, the man responded, 'It's here somewhere. Look, I was brought here last time and I can't remember what buzzer it is!'

'Well, is there no name?'

He turned, exasperated. 'No! Just a number. Then, in an undertone, 'Which I've forgotten.'

As Shane approached, the woman was saying, 'Well, why not ask someone?'

At this, the man looked very put out. Clearly, his cool evening out at an interesting after-hours was coming apart horribly. He turned on her and said, 'We can't. It's meant to be a secret, they might not let us in. Besides, not many people know about it.'

'Well it's better than hanging around here in the fog.'

Shane appraised the situation. The woman was quite attractive, if a little too much in the Camden fashion for his taste, and her fellow wouldn't look out of place, so he thought he could afford to be magnanimous.

'You going to Echopraxia?' he asked. 'It's just here.'

The relief on their faces was astounding. Anyone would have thought that Shane had saved the life of a close relative or at least rescued a beloved pet, whereas in reality he'd only shown them the entrance to an overrated shebeen. They followed him through the door once they'd been buzzed in, and offered him an array of twittering thanks and excuses.

'Couldn't remember the door, I was quite drunk last time.'

'I've heard about this place for ages.'

Shane soaked up their gratitude as he led them to the third floor bar. He was feeling worthy – no doors were barred to him – but there were few people inside to witness his triumphal entry. There will always be people who want to drink late in London during the week, the non-citizens, the irregularly employed or unemployed, those whose hours are out of keeping with the rest. Shane left his new chums at the bar and, picking up his drink, looked around for a table.

The interior resembled someone's flat, albeit one whose owner's taste ran to kitsch. Above the bar was an elk's head and huge old pictures of holiday destinations covered the walls. There was only one room but it snaked from the bar around a corner and past a small DJ area, so it gave the appearance of being at least two separate spaces. Shane moved into the more secluded section, where he found the film-maker (at least that's what his website said) Dean Jorden. He headed towards Dean, exclaiming, 'Hello mate how are you doing?'

Dean did his best to look pleased, smiled, scratched his head and said, 'Oh, so-so, I guess. Said I'd meet some people in here but it looks like they're not coming.' He fidgeted with his mobile. 'When did 'flaky' and 'flexible' become the same word?'

'Always the way, isn't it?' Shane replied cheerfully, sitting down.

'I said I'd meet Pearl here later, anyway. So here I am.' Dean settled back in as good an appearance of relaxation as the flimsy chair he was sitting on could afford. He was a large, ginger-haired man, whose formerly delicate features were being squeezed by an increasingly plump face.

'Things have been a bit like that of late,' he went on. 'A collection of no shows, half-completed projects, all very annoying. But once in a while something good comes off to keep the wolf from the door.'

Shane thought there was no danger of any wolf, except perhaps a particularly ambitious one, getting anywhere near Dean. At least Pearl would be there later, and maybe she'd have a friend with her, so Shane nodded sympathetically. Dean shifted his bulk in his seat and said, 'You know who you just missed?' Dean didn't wait for Shane to guess. 'Craig. He was all over that Claire from Norbury, that girl he works with.'

'That's a bit forward, isn't it? I thought he'd bought a flat with Fiona on his ill-gotten bonuses.'

'Ah, old story, I'm afraid,' said Dean. 'Fiona's off the scene and Craig doesn't seem bothered now he can see Claire openly. Talk about office snogging hour!'

Shane mused that it was only people who didn't work in offices that used the dismissive term to describe the salaried who got carried away after a few drinks and no food. He looked at Dean, never short of either, and tried to detect whether he really cared.

'Shame,' said Shane. 'I liked Fiona. A bit rough around the edges. And plump. But feisty. Always thought she'd be fantastic in bed.'

Dean responded coldly. 'If you say so. I think she was too much for Craig, either way. Didn't fit his idea of a metropolitan girlfriend, somehow. Kept hold of her provincial roots or whatever. Still, if Claire's the answer I'm really not sure about the question.'

ANOTHER REASON NOT TO GO TO CHELSEA

Okay, I'll see you later then… no, I guess I'll just go for a run.' What was that noise in the background? 'Yeah, gotta shift those pounds. Don't want to be seen with a taapie, do you?' There it was again – the sly movement of someone trying not to be overheard. 'Okay, hen. Cheerio.'

Fiona slipped the phone back into her pocket and regretted having dropped into regional dialect. Craig had found it charming once but she suspected it grated now, like her extra weight and any number of other vague irritations that he never mentioned but she was sure existed. Sometimes she thought it was just paranoia on her part and that things weren't so bad. However, she was no longer the fey Scottish pixie he'd first met five years before. Then again, neither was he the charming tractor boy from East Anglia. The two incomers had unquestionably been shaped by the city but, whereas Craig had morphed more into London she felt pushed out.

She was being squeezed in other ways too, out of her clothes mostly, and her jeans appeared to be involved in an ongoing struggle with her genes. The latter seemed determined to win out, despite her diet of salads and sushi (no meat and tatties), water and juices (no beer and whisky). Craig barely helped, with his pointed references to deep-fried Mars Bars and light-hearted ordering of pints of heavy on her behalf in pubs.

Fiona looked out of the window of the flat they'd bought together three years before. Beneath her was the splendour of Chelsea Bridge, the uprights' three supports resting on long, flat piers, the towers themselves resembling rockets ready for take off. If she leaned out of the window she could see the whole of her chosen route across Chelsea, along the north embankment, back over Albert Bridge and through the park. Hardly a marathon, but a decent start to her exercise regime. Soon, she planned to extend the loop out as far as the Battersea crossing. She glanced down and thought she saw a flicker of white on the foreshore between the two bridges before taking the stairs – not the lift – and jogging up to road level.

Halfway across the bridge, she caught sight of the white object again and realised that it was a huge horse cantering up and down the riverside. At first, she wondered whether something was being filmed along the embankment but there was no sign of a crew at road level. As she turned left at the end of the bridge, a small (closed) park blocked her view of the river.

She stopped at an iron ladder that led down to the river, and leaned over to peer down at the water. The horse had stopped running and was now idling along the shore. There was no one with the creature but suddenly it raised its ears and started running upriver at full pelt. Fiona followed from the higher level but couldn't keep up and by the time she had reached Albert Bridge it had disappeared. Crossing to the upriver side, she glanced down that way as well, but there was no sign of the animal; only a few hoof prints left in the Thames mud. After a few minutes, she carried on across the bridge and into Battersea Park, all the while keeping an eye on the northern shore, causing her almost to collide with another runner.

The following evening, Fiona paused by the ladder, hoping for another glimpse. At first, she didn't spot the young man with the camera, lounging against the embankment wall. It was possible that he'd been watching her for some time before he finally spoke.

'You've seen it as well, then?' Her heart jumped slightly, because his voice betrayed the unmistakable burr of the Highlands. She looked more closely at him and thought how beautiful he appeared, with the sinking sun blazing in the sky behind him. His blonde hair caught the rays and his loose casual clothes barely concealed a very athletic figure underneath. Only his smile was imperfect, truly Scottish in its jumbled disarray, but to Fiona even this possessed the charm of familiarity.

'I'm sorry... seen what?'

'You know, it's never here when I bring my camera. Total scunner.' He slung his camera to the side of his blue shirt and put out his hand. 'I'm Walter O'Hoy.'

She took it. 'Fiona Raasay. Nice to meet you.' Her accent slipped into a comfortable lowland brogue.

'Ah, paisan! Thought you couldn't be local, you're too friendly. How long have you been in exile?'

Fiona laughed. 'Feels like forever, but six years.'

'Still. At least it's voluntary, eh? Not like the poor sods that used to reside over there.' He indicated the grounds of the Chelsea Hospital over the road. Seeing her confusion, he smiled and explained. 'It was once was a jail for Scottish prisoners of war. Jacobites, Charlie's boys, speed bonnie et cetera. Typical English joke to make it the site of a flower festival, eh?'

His good humour was infectious and Fiona slipped into an easy conversation with him. As the two émigrés lounged against the wall, she told him about her work, her flat. She even intimated that things were not all that happy in her relationship, although part of her wanted him to think that there wasn't one. It was as if Walter had magically turned on a tap, out of which all her joys, sorrows, disappointments and triumphs since arriving in the city poured out.

Fiona wasn't even sure how much she told of her story in the city, or whether it had just raced through her mind, but Walter smiled and nodded and that was enough.

'It's no' easy in the great wen, is it? I love bits of London but I miss open space. I think that's why I come here so much. If you squint, all you can see is the river and trees of Battersea Park.'

'And the traditional rustic pagoda?' she asked.

'Yeah, that too.' He smiled as they both gazed at the golden statue in the white building across the water.

She learned that Walter had once studied photography at Chelsea Art College and spent a good deal of time photographing the park and riverside at night. As a result, he was full of knowledge about the area and, though his own tales were less personal than her own confessions, Fiona didn't care. She relaxed around him and enjoyed his daft sagas of the city. He told her about the lady cyclists who shocked people in the 1890s by riding through Battersea Park displaying their ankles, and Fiona wondered what the Victorians would make of the skimpy running shorts worn by women joggers today. Not Fiona, of course – she didn't feel that good about her thighs just at the moment. Of greater historical import (at least as Craig would have seen it) was that the first football match ever played under Football Association rules had taken place here in 1864.

They didn't talk about the horse. That was something they could return to at their leisure. They were both clearly interested in it, but Fiona was far keener to learn more about Walter at the moment than any white horse. She felt so strongly that they'd see each other again that she made the elementary mistake of not getting his phone number, only realising as she was jogging over Albert Bridge. She looked back to see him heading along Cheyne Walk.

Fiona's head had been turned by Walter's uncomplicated charm and his knowledge of the city. Five years, she'd been there, and she felt as if she knew nothing even about her own neighbourhood. She'd had no idea there had once been great Pleasure Gardens – Ranelagh and Cremorne - along the river here. That the river had been alive with boats and that the debauches on the banks had carried on all night. He had told her tales from the riverbank; how along the foreshore were remnants of religious services – Hindu, Christian, even Voodoo. In all honesty, he could have been talking about anything. Fiona had just loved how he expressed himself, and the unselfconscious way he flashed his shipwrecked dentistry.

Late nights at the office and an annoying weekend attending the wedding of one of Craig's colleagues meant that Fiona wasn't able to take her next evening run until the following Monday, a dreich night with rain whipping along the river and a gusty wind. Even Craig, who was at home preparing to watch his beloved Man United on TV, tried to talk her out of it. Quite aside from the possibility of seeing the horse or Walter, the prospect of Craig getting shouty and pointy in front of Sky Sports was enough to drive her out.

'You sure, love? It's the Scousers! Biggest game of the season.'

As she trotted down the stairs, Fiona remembered a Liverpudlian work colleague dismissively sneering that it might be, to people from East Anglia.

She dropped all thoughts of football as she headed over the bridge and at once saw the horse down on the foreshore, not far from where Walter had been standing the previous week. She hoped he was there and had got a photo of it. Well... she wished he was there, anyway. The horse cantered downstream then abruptly turned round and went back the other way. Fiona increased her pace, keeping her eyes on the white shape as well as she could while avoiding the inevitable hazards of the London pavement – blowing plastic bags, discarded brollies and wet pulped newspapers.

When she could see down to the river once more, the horse was gone. She dawdled briefly by the iron ladder before the rain became too intense. As a sort of mantra to cover her disappointment she thought of the famous exiles that had once lived in Cheyne Walk, and imagined herself following in their footsteps: George Eliot, to George Best, Henry James to James Whistler. This also prevented her from thinking inappropriate thoughts about Walter and resentful ones about Craig. Looking back from the centre of Albert Bridge, she thought she saw a glimpse of white on the foreshore, at the entrance of what appeared to be a cave in the embankment wall. She didn't stand long, though, as the rain was lashing up the river, and she was grateful to reach the relative shelter afforded by the park's trees.

She was drenched and windswept by the time she reached her block (designed, apparently, to enhance the natural environment and quality of life). As she headed for the shower, she could hear Craig singing a song about Scousers eating rats.

The following evening she was luckier, at least in one regard, because Walter was at his spot by the ladder, camera hoisted. She ran up to him, smiling, checking herself from throwing her arms around him. After all, they had only met once.

'Did you get a picture?' she cried.

'Hello, my Caledonian lovely. Yes I did, but you've just missed it. And I've missed you the last week. Where have you been?'

Fiona told him that she had seen the horse the previous night, finishing by saying, 'I thought I saw something in that place that looks like a cave, but I wasn't sure.'

'It's where the river Westbourne enters the Thames. It's a sort of storm sewer tunnel. Gets you all the way up to the Serpentine.

Part of it flows through Sloane Square Tube station in a pipe.' He paused and looked upriver before continuing. 'I don't think that's how the horse gets down there, though. There are entrances down by Battersea Bridge, I think it uses those. Or rather, I think someone leads it down from there and lets it run along the river at low tide. It probably belongs to some rich eccentric.' He trailed off. 'Impressed that you made it last night. That's commitment!'

'Well, you know. Got to get trim!' She blushed, then laughed. 'Maybe riding would help. I used to love riding when I was a child.'

He looked confused, and let his eyes linger over her curves. 'Well you look pretty slim to me,' he said. There was a slight pause after this, which Walter filled by suggesting they walk along the river bank. He had to leave, he said, but he thought he knew when the horse might appear the next evening. 'Try to be there at seven, down on the foreshore. Tide should be right then, plenty of room for it.'

He waved to her from the end of Albert Bridge as she sauntered towards the park.

Fiona rushed through her work the next day, to make sure she would be home in good time to get to the river for seven. This had occasioned a rather brusque conversation with Craig, who was going to a drinks do at Leadenhall Market. It had ended, from her point of view, with the words, 'Well they're your friends, not mine, and I'm sure Claire will keep you company, at least. I'll see you later.'

There was no sign of Walter or anyone else as she pounded along the embankment, winter taking a bite out of the autumn evening. It was odd how little used this section of riverfront was, except during the Chelsea flower show and Guy Fawkes Night, when this stretch provided the best (free) vantage point for the fireworks in Battersea Park. She reached the ladder and paused to look down. The tide was out, leaving an expanse of mud, sand and stones. There was still no sign of Walter, although he could have been delayed, of course. She waited a minute before swinging herself onto the embankment and starting the twenty-foot descent, being careful not to look down.

When she felt her feet touch the soft ground, her first thought was to wonder whether it was legal for her to be there. She was sure that no drivers had paid any attention to her going over the wall. It was possible to be seen from the park and the bridges, but she thought it unlikely that anyone would look. Then she saw the horse. It stood just past the entrance to the Westbourne.

Fiona sidled up to it and began caressing its head. The horse wore no bridle, but she knew that many animals had microchips under their skin as proof of identity. She felt along the creature's neck for evidence of one and as she did this, the horse lowered its neck, almost, she felt, inviting her to mount it. It had been years since she had ridden a horse and she felt incredibly self-conscious. She was also a little fearful that someone would turn up. But the horse seemed to be pleading with her to climb on his back, making soft whinnies and nudging her. After a final glance around, Fiona climbed on, grabbing its mane to keep her balance. Once there, however, she felt solidly in place, as if something adhesive on the horse's back was keeping her on. This was reassuring because, as soon as she was comfortable, the horse began to canter upstream along the sand, gathering speed as they headed towards Albert Bridge. Just before the bridge, it turned rapidly and galloped in the other direction. Fiona felt the rush of the wind as they hurtled along the foreshore, her inner thighs tingling where they dug in for greater grip. She felt free and alive and more exhilarated than she had done for years. This was like a first kiss, or the rush of a drug or a dizzying revelation of beauty.

It was fantastic, just like flying. The horse fled underneath Chelsea Bridge and beyond, to where the water started opposite the empty hulk of Battersea Power Station. Downriver, Fiona could see the lights of south London glimmering. Across the water, the top floor of her block was visible above the trains snailing the last few hundred yards to Victoria or scurrying, liberated, towards the junction and the coast beyond. Turning west, the horse tore along the sand and stone of the exposed riverbed, sending wading birds, come to feed in the exposed pools, flapping off over the water.

Fiona was ecstatic. As they headed back for Battersea Bridge, her hair flew and her thighs gripped tightly, and she thought she could hear a song that seemed familiar.

'I never thought it would happen with a Scots girl from Clapham.' The voice seemed to coming from beneath her, but that was absurd. It had to be coming from somewhere on the river. The song continued. She looked down, and the horse turned its head towards her. It was his teeth she recognised first.

'I knew you'd come, my Caledonian lovely. I knew you'd come. And admit it – it was me you wanted to ride all along, eh?'

With a scream, she tried to dismount but found herself glued to the horse's back. Faster and faster he galloped along the foreshore, finally belting into the cave and under the water, beneath the soupy swirl of the river.

Craig had not gone home the previous night, and assumed that was why Fiona was ignoring his calls. After his fourth attempt, he picked up the Standard and was oddly arrested by a headline on page three that read; 'Human liver found in Serpentine'.

ECHO OF THE PAST

IN HIS COMMENTS ABOUT FIONA, SHANE SENSED THAT HE MIGHT have said the wrong thing. But that's what journalists do, he thought – we're blunt and we ask awkward questions. So he compounded his first error by next asking Dean, 'Do you still keep in contact with Mr Timotny at all? It's just that I'm going to a preview of his tomorrow, a film called An Estate of Mind. I've got the invite here.'

He took a card from his pocket and handed it to Dean, who glanced at it. It bore some rather fanciful pictures of urban decay, with three faces staring from it and a great deal of text in the centrefold. Dean began to read it aloud, laughing every now and then.

' "Cracked concrete casements. Words fall from a psychology book. Depraved, deprived, depressed, twisted, torn, tangled, the DTs of modern living. Mr Timotny's bold film takes us to where dirty sinks do not work and fungal growths nest in the broken faucets." Well – he always was a bit rubbish domestically… "Across the hall, a scout party of cockroaches have taken up residence and there are rumours of rats as big as cats, and squirrels dealing crack from the non-trees of the estate." '

He paused for a few seconds. 'Well, this is certainly upbeat for him. What has he done, Wind in the Willows for the roof-rack generation?' Dean lit a cigarette, coughed, and added, 'Mind you, it's taken him long enough. He was already doing it when I was sharing a flat with him in Acton.'

'So he's persevered then,' said Shane.

Behind his cloud of smoke, Dean had returned to the flyer. 'Oh the little git, that's one of my lines! "All the youth have bobbies and the grass outside is fed on a diet of chips and beer cans, thereby giving it an environmental balance with its human neighbours."

Bobby D'Avro, ASBO, he'd never have thought that up.'

Dean's face creased into a smile and he shrugged. 'I'll say one thing for him. William Timotny is certainly tenacious when it comes to getting his truth out there, even if it isn't actually his truth.'

Stubbing out his cigarette, he said, 'All my info about William is second-hand these days. But I hope he does well with it. Ah, Arts Council funding! Wonder how he got that?'

'So you're not exactly best mates any more, then?' prompted Shane. Dean didn't reply, so, thinking it might make an interesting angle for his review of William's film, Shane continued to fish.

'You left the flat for reasons of artistic difference?' he guessed.

'Huh,' Dean snorted. 'That's one way of putting it.' He smiled and looked at Shane, reminding himself what he was talking to before carrying on. 'There's not much to tell really, no big story. We were working on different things and I was starting to get commercial film work. Then Pearl's dad bought her a flat in Bethnal Green and I moved there with her.'

'So what did William do?'

Dean began playing with his phone again. 'Timotny? He stayed over Acton way somewhere. Got himself a bunch of acolytes and kept on doing what he always did.' Dean seemed a little preoccupied, but added, 'I think he used to fancy Pearl a lot at one point. That sort of thing's always hard to gauge with him, but I think he might have seen it as a sort of betrayal when I got together with her. That was her texting just now, she should be here in a minute. She'll be interested to see that invite too.'

'Good,' said Shane. 'I need a word with her about her mate Mr London. So what else have you got going on?'

'Me? I had a great thing set up with Steve Granger from Herne Hill, but he's vanished. First whiff of the US dollar and he's over there to make a feature, something about sex toys. So I've gone back to pop promo stuff, a bit of corporate work. It pays well but, you know, it's not as satisfying as doing your own material, but anything of my own will have to wait for more finance.'

Dean took a swig from his bottle and laughed. 'You know, I went to a networking thing in Soho earlier, trying to sniff out some finance, and I'm too soft when it comes to selling myself.' He looked down at his expanding waistline as he said this. 'There were too many shiny-suited tigers telling their stories, flogging their wares.' Dean was lost for a moment as he summoned up the memory, then restarted. 'Honestly, though. You should have heard some of the rubbish being pitched. Salsa zombie movies – the dance, not the sauce. Silly heist capers. I couldn't even drink my way through it, the beer was £4.50 a bottle!'

Shane said, 'I thought everyone had at least one silly crime caper in them. You know, people once met in places like this to plot heists. Now we just sit around talking about making films about them. Hard to say which is more criminal really.'

'Well. Some might say that what the Arts Council does is pretty larcenous.' Dean paused then said. 'I heard another bit of good news from the art and crime interface. You know that shop that trades on Brazilian ghetto culture?'

Shane nodded so Dean continued. 'They got done over the other day. A team came down from Dalston with shooters and made off with everything. One of the owners started bleating that they should be ripping off big business instead of small ones.' Dean snorted slightly as his beer went down the wrong way. 'Anyway, this Dalston geezer slaps him and says, "Welcome to the real favela culture wanker" and sambaed backwards out of the place.'

Shane smiled, 'Bet William would have loved to have filmed that.'

LONDON AFTER MIDNIGHT
(SOME YEARS PREVIOUSLY)

Thousands of people were swarming like flies around Notting Hill underground, many of them carrying bags, boxes and the smug expression that is worn by the happy shopper. The Saturday market was over for the week; had, in fact, been over for a few hours, leaving behind it the mashed fruit, soiled clothes, empty packaging and spilt wares that were yet to be cleaned up. The people remaining were those who had hung around for a snack, a coffee or something stronger, chatting to friends, browsing the shops near the tube that stayed open later and generally having a really enjoyable, proper Saturday in West London. No doubt some of them were looking forward to going home, trying on some of their purchases and having an equally enjoyable proper Saturday night out in west London, or wherever they came from.

Only a short distance away were some of the criminals, hustlers and vagabonds that gravitate towards London's markets; and also William Timotny. William's contribution to London's shadow economy this Saturday had been selling questionable films at one of his jobs, behind the counter at Aguesta Video in Soho. Before that, he had spent a long Friday night editing his own 'latest' (and so far only) film. Now he glowered outside the Coronet Cinema, watching the stragglers make their way home past the sharks and scanning the crowd in vain for his friends.

'Bloody Pearl! Bloody Dean! Bloody typical!' he rumbled. 'Just because they've got mobiles, they think they can disregard arrangements. I told them the film starts at 7pm!'

Practically all of his friends had mobile phones now but William didn't and held onto a number of negative theories about them. His most frequently voiced opinion, and one that he polished in his head now, was that, genetically, they were bad for the species. His argument ran that, in the not too distant past, if two stupid people made an arrangement to meet, there was a decent chance of them screwing it up, as meeting required a sense of time and geography, and a modicum of forward planning. But not any more. How many times had he heard, while standing outside the National Film Theatre on the South Bank, variations of the following conversation:

'Where are you? I'm by the bookstand! Sorry I'm late.'

'So am I. I can see you, I'm by the far table, waving.'

'Me too, I'm waving as well.'

And sure enough, there would be a pair of cheery loons waving. Technology had facilitated the meeting of this pair of dullards, with the result that there was now a possibility of them starting a long-term relationship and going on to procreate. Naturally enough, any children born of such a union stood a good chance of being at least as dense as their parents. Thus, the human gene pool would be diminished. There was no need for super-computers to take over, or for evil thinking bombs; the malign influence of even the simplest technology was plain enough to see.

It wasn't just technology that vexed William; he had a whole grocer's store of resentments and frustrations. Near the top of his list were currently sex (lack of) and relationships (unsure of). Although he wasn't entirely clear how exactly these were linked, he knew there was a crossover somewhere. He'd seen it at the movies. On a more specifically personal point, he was annoyed at the amount of time Pearl and Dean were spending together and the fact that they had gone to the vintage film fair at the Guildhall that afternoon, while he'd had to go to work.

Dean and he had been collaborating on projects since film school, where their short (entitled 'Lava Lamp') had been highly commended. A friendly, ginger-haired man, Dean smoothed out some of William's more radical ideas and made them work.

Pearl was a relatively recent arrival on the scene, having answered their advert for a flatmate in September. Dean and William had been very specific in the advert: *Reservoir Dogs require Uma. Preferably non-smoker.* She had certainly started out well, from William's POV. Her father had been something in the old Rank Organisation and what she didn't know about Hammer wasn't worth considering. The three of them quickly formed the North Acton Film Society and Production Company and in the ensuing months had spent happy times trawling the capital's charity stores for equipment. They made frequent visits to outlying repertory cinemas and were no strangers to the underground screenings of Reg Action and the Tushingham Cinema Committee, which took them to all manner of strange, often abandoned, buildings across the capital.

There was a time when Pearl's wool-clad legs and blonde hair, covered by her jaunty beret, had inspired lascivious thoughts in William. These days he was less enamoured, and now he reconsidered her, as he stood outside the old Coronet in what he hoped might be mistaken for a Shaft-like pose. To a squint-eyed admirer, he might just come across as a plump Richard Roundtree in his leather coat, shouty scarf and dark Levis. He swivelled round again, thinking that, cinematically, Pearl had a rather weak face.

With no sight of either Pearl's face or Dean weaving through the crowds, William gave up and headed into the Coronet. There was a low turnout for a Saturday night, and he settled himself near the front, in centre left of the row. At least there wouldn't be the traditional argument about which position in the theatre was best to view the film from. Dean preferred the middle, Pearl liked the back and William had to have the screen right on top of him. He had got there first so they would have to accept his choice, and if they cared to, they'd know where to look.

Casting this rather bitter thought aside, he cut to thinking about his current project, Holly Street: An Estate of Mind. It was a study of beauty and decay set on a blasted council scheme in North East London, weaving together a group of young people's lives. An enigmatic Afro-Saxon filmmaker, a character based rather fancifully on William's own, linked the stories. While he was pleased with that personality, he thought some of the others could be a bit more credible. He had been putting in long hours on the film over the past few months, as well as his paying jobs. This, and the warmth of the Coronet, resulted in his dozing off.

When he came to William noticed that the cinema seemed emptier than before, and he wondered how much he had missed. The sight of an usherette passing up the aisle reassured him that a film was still to be shown and he hoped it would be the promised surprise feature. The screen came to life, and William blinked when, accompanied by the sort of dramatic organ sound not produced this side of World War Two, the grainy title appeared. In large white letters against a pitch-black background, it read: London After Midnight. William stared in surprise; this film was legendary.

All tiredness banished, he devoured the images, paying attention to nothing else, except happy thoughts of how annoyed Dean would be to have missed this. To any film obsessive, London After Midnight was Shangri La. Made in 1927 by Tod Browning, it was now rivalled only by the long version of Erich von Stroheim's Greed as the most famous of all 'lost' films. London After Midnight starred Lon Chaney Senior, with Conrad Nagel, Polly Moran and Henry B Walthall supporting. The plot had Chaney's character, a dapper vampire with wild hair, living with a bevy of female companions in the London mansion of Roger Balfour, a supposed suicide. He was pitted against a Scotland Yard detective whose unorthodox methods eventually solve the mystery of Roger Balfour's death.

There had always been rumours in the film underground that a mysterious private collector held a copy. Legend had it that Blackhawk Film's 1973 catalogue had London After Midnight on offer. Another story was that a local 16mm film society showed the film in 1975, scotching tales that the last prints were destroyed in a vault fire in the 1960s. But the last reviews from credible witnesses were from the 1950s.

William settled back – after all, there was ample room to do so – and basked in his extreme good fortune. There was no doubt that Lon Chaney was excellent as the lead. He would have been perfect as Dracula in the film Tod Browning directed two years later, had he not by then contracted cancer. The later film was eventually distinguished by the fact that its Castle Dracula was home to armadillos instead of rats. It was filmed at the same time as a Mexican version, and on the same set; the Mexicans used armadillos to add a little local colour and when Browning saw their rushes he decided to put the unlikely creatures in his version too.

Information like this came easily to William, who had the mind of a hoarder. His head was an over-stuffed attic of film trivia and cross-references that enabled him to make swift comparisons and improbable juxtapositions of cinematic styles that, he liked to think, were the envy of his friends. He could see pretty quickly, for example, that this was not the classic that it laid claim to be. Whether he would share this information was another matter; there would always be the temptation to enhance the picture's qualities in order to make his night seem all the more spectacular.

He sat while the final credits rolled, then, reluctantly, left his seat. He could see that he was the last person in there, apart from the diminutive usherette.

As he stood shivering, waiting for the bus, William wondered whether the usherette had been a kindred spirit, so obsessed by film that little else mattered, and regretted that he hadn't asked her out. Before he could act on this thought, the N94 appeared.

It had gone 2am when he entered the kitchen, disturbing a solitary mouse that had been having a fine time with a discarded packet of Doritos. What was it about rodents and their adolescent diets, he wondered, helping himself to the remains of a bottle of Bulgarian red that the mouse hadn't bothered with.

William woke at around eleven to find the pair of them already up. Had he been paying attention, he might have noticed a curious furtiveness about their behaviour, a particular closeness masquerading as its opposite. It was William could have spotted immediately in a film but this was real life.

'So what happened to you two last night, then, eh?' he said. Magnanimously, he thought, because after all, what could have compared to the evening he'd had?

'What happened to us?' Pearl, again. 'What happened to you?'

'Me? I was in the cinema. As arranged.' This did jar slightly. 'Where do you think I was?'

'Well, mate, hard to tell.' This was Dean now. His tone was conciliatory. 'We were waiting for you outside the Coronet when it emptied, and it's not like you're hard to spot is it?'

'We thought we'd take you for a drink. Make up for not making it to the film.' This time he caught something in Pearl's tone.

'And to tell you… what's going on,' said Dean. William was too full of his own news to notice their exchanged glances. 'We got caught at the film fair,' Dean continued. 'We've got some great stuff to show you later.'

'Then the bloody tube, there was a bomb scare, which left us stuck and by the time we got to the cinema it was too late. Obviously we couldn't phone you,' added Pearl, pointedly.

William couldn't have cared less – he wasn't interested in their excuses, although he was secretly pleased they'd been delayed. It sounded like they hadn't exactly had a great time.

'Well, your loss,' he told them. 'I stayed for the special late feature. You won't believe what it was…' He recounted his evening, adding some bonus footage, DVD extra scenes featuring the usherette. Eventually, Dean broke in.

'But there was no late feature. The cinema closed for repairs last night after the last show ended at nine o'clock, there was a sign up and everything. We waited outside, like Pearl said. '

'Look,' said Pearl. 'Call them up.' She punched a few buttons on her mobile and handed it to William.

He took the phone and, after a couple of rings, heard a woman's voice say, 'Thank you for calling the Notting Hill Coronet Cinema. We will be closed for refurbishment from 9pm on Saturday the fourteenth of February until 7pm on Monday the first of March. When we reopen…'

William dropped the phone and looked at his erstwhile comrades. He noticed they were holding hands.

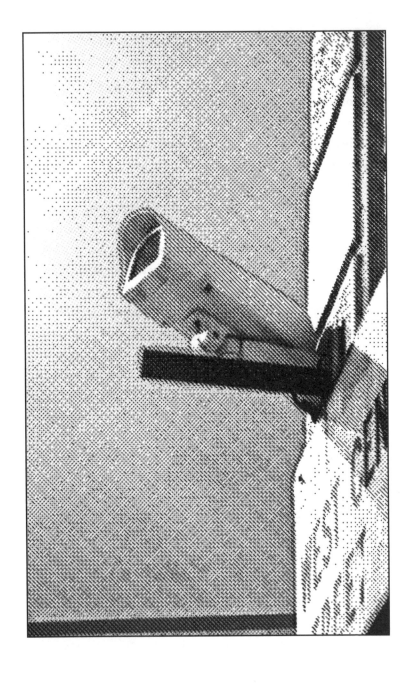

FRESH ARRIVALS IN ECHO

SHANE SLIPPED OFF TO THE TOILETS AND WHEN HE RETURNED, A blonde woman had joined Dean.

'Hiya Pearl, how are you? Working late?' Shane stooped down and made a point of kissing her.

Looking slightly distracted and adjusting her appearance in a small mirror, the woman said, 'Yeah, I've been editing some material we shot in the summer for a Halloween special. Bit of a bust, in a lot of ways. We've got loads of footage and the woman we were interviewing speaks with a lovely voice but uses this weird slang.'

Pearl's clipped tones managed to prevent this from coming out in one long gush, as she fumbled across the table for one of Dean's cigarettes. Once this was lit, she returned to her mirror and said, 'Urgh! I look a right mess!' before producing a make-up bag and starting to sort out her look.

To anyone else, Pearl would have come across as perfectly fine, glamorous even, but a few years in front of the camera had given her an awareness of the tricks that it could pull and had altered, perhaps forever, Pearl's own vision of herself.

'She foreign? The woman you were interviewing?' asked Shane.

Pearl looked up mid-dab and said, 'No, might as well have been but no, bloody cockney. Well family from the West Indies back in the day, but a London something, definitely.' She took a drag and exhaled. 'Either of you any idea what cuntipotent means?'

'What?' This came from both of them.

'C-U-N-T-I-P-O-T-E-N-T. It means having all things. Good word, eh?' Pearl smiled, sipped at her drink and glanced around the bar. It was still a thinnish crowd, both in number and body type but as the bar didn't close until two there was always the chance of fresh arrivals. Despite the relaxed atmosphere, quite a lot of business got done here, or at least that's what the regulars liked to think. Certainly, quite a lot of rumours got started, and any number of ill-advised ideas were brought to fruition by the combination of youth, money, know-nothing confidence and proximity. Shane spotted the couple that had come in with him talking to a former reality show contestant and was certain that was the case there.

Wondering whether he could do a feature on Pearl's programme, Shane asked what its background was.

'Oh, it's a bunch of spooky tales. London ghost stories and what have you, 15-minute slots. Princes in towers, 19th century nurses still patrolling hospital wards, strange beasties and odd happenings.' She snapped into life a bit, realising that Shane might be able to give the programme a decent mention and added, 'I can e-mail you the details if you like, or I've a version on my phone. We'd hoped to get something supernatural on camera – you know, an actual phantom – but no such luck.'

'What happens in the one you were working on tonight?'

'It's a kind of murder-repeating story, near Tavistock Square. I got my mate Emma Louise in as a cultural commentator for it.'

'How is she?' asked Dean.

'Emma? Oh she's fine. Quite the consummate media professional. I don't know whether academics get training those days or whether it just comes from delivering talks all the time. Told me a great story about the junkie ballet of Camden.'

'What is it, some sort of outreach programme?' Asked Shane.

'No these are real people, addicts and dealers. They pirouette and twist up the High Street, taking very precise steps and making abrupt turns and leaps. It's not art exactly , they're doing it to avoid the CCTV by moving in the spaces the cameras don't reach. The blank spots they've learned by rumour, experience and cunning.'

Both men laughed. Shane asked what exactly Emma Louise did, and Pearl apologised: 'Oh, sorry, I thought you knew her. She studies urban legends. You know – modern fairy stories. The story we were filming sort of fitted into that area.'

Pearl attached an earpiece to her phone and passed it to Shane, who stared down at the screen.

He watched as a title sequence emerged from a dark backdrop, ending with the words 'The Brothers' Square Dance'. Pearl appeared, talking directly to camera, which pulled away to reveal her location in a city square.

'Hello, I'm Pearl Dawson. Welcome to the second part of One Eye Grey, a series of programmes that sets out to explore some of the stranger stories that London has to offer. In the first programme we concentrated on South London but tonight we are here in North Bloomsbury, a quiet area despite its proximity to the British Museum, and Euston and Kings Cross Stations. It is home to the London University and has strong connections with London's literary set.'

Images of various novelists and writers including Coleridge, Hazlett and Lamb flashed across the screen as Pearl continued, 'Some describe the area as Hamilton Country, after the novelist Patrick Hamilton, but it is more popularly associated with Virginia Woolf and the Bloomsbury group. It is interest in her that draws sensibly shod walking tours to this part of London.'

The camera panned around the area to give viewers a good look at the location.

'It is unlikely that those writers of fiction could conceive of a tale as strange as the one we have for you. Though perhaps Mary Shelley, who was born just the other side of the Euston Road, comes the closest. But before we start on tonight's peculiar tale, I'd like to introduce Emma Louise Tennant of London University to give us some background.'

The camera focused on a tall, dark-haired woman wearing a silk scarf, very fashionable glasses and a pale blue trouser suit. She was standing confidently in front of a bench and smiling at the camera. Lettering across the screen gave her name and profession, though it was too small to read, and Shane regretted that the image of Emma wasn't better. Pearl was talking again.

'Emma Louise, your job title is Head of Modern Myth Studies. What exactly does that mean?'

The dark-haired woman smiled and looked into the camera. 'The essence of modern myth studies is the investigation of contemporary, mostly urban, stories and what these tales tell us about present-day society. We are accustomed to using the chronicles of ancient cultures to provide an insight into those cultures' way of life, and the stories I look into offer a means of analysing our own.'

She paused briefly and turned slightly to her right as the camera panned over to take in the University College of London building.

'Not only do the stories themselves reveal a great deal but also the manner in which they are told and the groups in society that are receptive to them. For example, my own name is more interesting to some undergraduates in my college than it might be elsewhere. Not because of me, but because there is a belief among them that if you say Emma Louise three times in front of mirrors in the building, the ghost of a student called Emma Louise will appear.'

'Astonishing!' said Pearl, in faux amazement. 'Who was other Emma?'

'She was a student who died – allegedly – whilst studying at University College London, late in the 20th century,' came the smiling reply as Emma removed her glasses.

'You said allegedly. What does that mean?'

The camera had stayed on Emma Louise, who was clearly enjoying herself.

'Just that there's no record of a student called Emma Louise. But the legend has taken root and, in the manner of these things, will probably never go away. There are many more such tales on American University campuses and it appears that the UCL one is a direct migration from there. It shows, if you like, how entwined the British and US cultures are.'

'I see. But you have a much more unique and specifically London story that takes or took place in this square?'

'That's right and, unusually, it's something we are able to witness first hand.' The camera switched to other side of the square, where Emma Louise was not standing. The effect was of a ghostly disappearance, intended to jolt the audience. Emma reappeared abruptly, and continued talking as she strolled across the square. At least, Shane assumed that was what was going on. It was hard to tell on the tiny monitor.

'I first became aware of Josephine Campbell a couple of summers ago and although I didn't know her name at the time, she was very hard to miss. I was sitting right here and I could see this immaculately dressed black lady, apparently hopping around. On closer inspection, I realised that she was doing a complicated series of dance steps.'

As Emma was talking, music began to play and the screen was filled with the image of a woman performing a highly ritualised dance. Occasionally, she would drop a flower and say a few words. Once or twice, she seemed to miss her footing on an invisible step, and ruefully apologised.

The camera returned to Pearl, who said, 'That was Josephine Campbell. We'll be talking to her in a minute but first, Emma Louise, you believe that ghosts are beings that move in the spaces most of us don't see. The dark corners and hidden recesses, the cracks in the pavement, if you like.'

'I'm not sure I believe that, but it is one explanation offered. Most people can't see this phenomenon but Josephine believes she can see something. What she is doing is re-enacting the last movements of two dear friends of hers, who died in the square. She was there at the time of the tragedy, and witnessed it. In a sense, hers is a memorial dance to the dead. This is common in some cultures but unusual in London, certainly in such a public place.

'But there is more to Josephine's dance than that, as we are about to find out. I'd like to introduce Josephine Campbell.'

The picture cut to an impressively dressed lady, possibly in her thirties, looking rather severely into the camera. The overall effect of her clothing stunned the viewer in its collision of colours, layers and fabrics, as if she had wanted to wear all her best clothes at once. She stood very still and waited for her questions.

'Ms Campbell, can you tell us the background to your dancing in the square?'

The lady seemed to freeze, then took a deep breath and started talking. She was quite nervous but clearly determined, and spoke in a beautiful lilting voice that enunciated every word precisely, even if some of the words were unfamiliar.

At this point Shane lost interest because Emma Louise, who was exactly the sort of clever looker Shane went one-handed surfing for, was no longer on the screen. He pulled out the earpiece and said to Pearl, 'That looks good. What's the story behind it?'

Pearl took back her phone, checked there were no new messages and said, 'There is a legend that, in the long ago and far away, two brothers fought a duel and died on the fields that now make up Tavistock Square; for decades afterwards, people saw their footprints appearing.' She lit a cigarette and asked, 'With me so far?'

Shane and Dean both nodded, so Pearl continued. 'Well, Josephine, the woman in our film, claims to be seeing another set of footprints. These are of two brothers – whether blood or other – who were killed in the 1990s. This pair checked out fighting over a right sort by the name of Estella, who was shagging both of them, and Josephine witnessed the fight. According to Josephine things ended badly for Estella, in a fire at a crack house a few years later.'

'Now, I've warned you about that before,' came a voice. 'It's a ghetto drug, darlings.'

The interruption had come from a sleepy-looking woman in a floaty ensemble of dresses and wraps, who was drifting gracefully towards their table. At a distance she appeared to be in a bit of a daze but once closer, her eyes were alive with a quick intelligence and good humour.

Shane looked up and said, 'Hiya, Sophie. I saw your cousin James on telly the other night. Become quite a pest, hasn't he? Is he about to become the new official opposition?'

Sophie smiled, playing with a distinctive silver pendant around her neck and said, 'Hard to say, really. I think my mum's more proud of him for resigning than she was when he got the job in the first place. My auntie's a bit worried, though. She's got it into her head that the dirty tricks department is about to give him a going over. She thinks someone's going to give his story to the papers.' She glanced lazily at Shane as if she might have something to add.

'You don't think it was anything that was said at your birthday meal do you?' said Shane. 'Everyone was very critical of the government that night.'

'I wouldn't flatter yourself on that. Though you got some mileage out of being there, didn't you?' She concentrated hard to remember. 'Politician Pizza Off', wasn't it? That your own headline, was it?'

Shane smiled and admitted it wasn't. 'But yes, they let me cover the story on the strength of that, the regular political writer was furious. Anything else I should know? Anything sordid from James Daly MP's youth waiting to emerge?'

Sophie shifted her flimsy skirt beneath her as she swept her legs onto the sofa, revealing in the process an astoundingly costly pair of shoes and some expressive hosiery. Enjoying the effect this had on the three of them, she leaned over and whispered, 'Well, darlings. There was one incident with a girlfriend of his. And her dog. This was before he came out, obviously. Draw closer and I'll tell all.'

They drew in as Sophie swept her hair from her face and began. 'James was very shy in his youth. He was self-conscious when he got his first girlfriend, which is understandable, all things considered. Anyway, she was a good sport called Carly, from a big family who had a couple of dogs that they all doted on.' Sophie glanced around conspiratorially before continuing.

'So James is invited around to meet the family. He's a bit nervous but settles down on the sofa, he's introduced to the mum and dad and the two sisters and the brother, but none of them are making much of an effort to talk to him. They're just playing with the dogs or sitting in silence. Well, of course, James is getting more and more nervous. All his attempts at conversation are floundering and he's starting to panic. So he's casting around the room for something to comment on and spots one of the dogs bent over, licking its own balls.' Sophie's posh voice, modified over the years from its Midlands' original, was perfect for swearing because even the most innocuous word sounded naughty. The three listeners strained harder to hear.

'Well, in his panic, James points at the dog and blurts out, 'I wish I could do that!' This is met with silence until one of the sisters says, 'Well, give him a biscuit and he might let you.' Sophie burst out laughing, Shane groaned and the others slowly began to giggle. When she had recovered, Sophie said, 'Well honestly, what were you expecting, you mucky pups? He is in the Labour party, not the Conservatives!'

Then she said, 'Whenever he gets a really savage putdown in the House, he says he always grades it against that incident. He told me it had taught him many things. That uncomfortable silence is sometimes the best thing. That it's better to keep your mouth shut and appear stupid than open it and prove it. And finally, that the dog's bollocks are always the dog's bollocks.'

'Eh? What does that mean?' asked Dean.

'Oh, I think he lets it mean many things, darling, but probably that we're responsible for our own reputation in the end. And that the dog can clean its own balls or, indeed, that the government can cover its own balls-up. Cheers!'

She took a swallow of her drink, still laughing at her own story.

THE LORD PROTECTOR HAS HIS SAY

Hot in the city, tense as in the aftermath of a crime and loose in the expectation of summer. What is a man to do on an evening like this but drink in the lovelies with their warm-weather wardrobes, and swallow beer? Everyone is still busy, of course, but rarely, except in the summer, does London really do that work hard/play hard thing properly. In the winter (nine months), it's closer to work hard /struggle against the temptation to stay at home eating chocolate and boozing. In June, July and August, and occasionally a few weeks either side, everything takes to the streets. The pubs overflow and develop potbellies of revellers around their entrances, staying late because the liquor has engendered a careless optimism that, of course, Transport For London will get them home.

So it was that James Daly, Home Office Under Secretary and Member for Birmingham Sutton Coldfield found himself a bit lit, a spot late and a tad off message, wandering east from St Giles towards Holborn underground station. Fresh threats were facing the capital and he had been helping to frame crisp legislation to counter them. Even so, he would never have missed his favourite cousin's birthday. It had been held in a brash but nevertheless inexpensive Italian on New Oxford Street. One of her guests, that annoying hack Shane Satey, had told everyone that the restaurant had been built on the site of a café that had been Orwell's inspiration for the Chestnut Tree caff in 1984. James thought he'd heard the same story about the

McDonalds a few doors down but didn't venture this option because he had enough arguments in the House of Commons without disagreements spilling into Sophie's birthday.

It had got him thinking, though, being a political animal, about the nature of Britain in the new century. Italian restaurants themselves could hardly be described as novel, particularly in this part of London, but the fact that they only served Italian dishes was a fresh twist. Until relatively recently, egg, chips and bacon would have featured on the menu, along with other dishes unknown in Tuscany or Sicily, such as steak and kidney pie. Now they were less batter and more ciabatta. James liked this progress and refused to sanction the theory that choice was diminishing on the restaurant front, with Starbucks and McDonalds spreading American tastes (and waistlines) across the globe. As far as he could remember, it wasn't much more than a decade ago that there were only four cafes in the whole of London that served decent coffee. He wondered what Orwell would make of all the changes, as Orwell had always paid a great deal of attention to food.

James had read most of Orwell's work by an embarrassingly young age and though he hadn't understood it all as a youngster, he had returned to the texts over and over again throughout his life. Had Orwell not died so young their lives would have overlapped slightly, though James was most interested in what Orwell would have made of the 21st century. He was confident that he would have liked the food and coffee, though probably not the prices. What might he have made of the TV programme Big Brother, and the omnipresence of CCTV, though? Would Orwell think he had got the future right? And, as in 1984, James thought, we did seem to be creating a state of perpetual war and fear.

Debating such issues across the dispatch boxes was James's trade.

He provided the facts to support policy and keep it on course. He was certain that he wasn't the only one within the government who was having doubts about the drift of its strategy. As yet, he hadn't voiced these concerns, however, beyond his constituency chairman and immediate family. It was like coming out: tell those you trust most first. Sophie's birthday certainly hadn't been the time for indiscreet counter briefings and he knew that Shane hadn't been the only scrivener present. Of course, it was said that in London you were never more than a few feet away from a journalist. It was only natural that several of the gathering had tried to prise information out of him or engage him in discussion. 'But, really, can't we just stop bullying other countries?' one equine ponce had whinnied. Another, more seriously, had expressed that he was a freeborn Briton and needed no chit for permission to walk where he liked in his own bloody country. Where James had thought the former laughably adolescent, he had sympathy for the latter.

James had entered politics to be tough on the causes of inequality, not tough on the cause of liberty. All night, he had been trying to remember a line from Kipling's poem The Reeds of Runnymede. He was concerned that, in the long term, such an authoritarian policy would harm the Labour party's electoral prospects. He knew how a single small piece of legislation could damage a party, the way that Section 28, had wrecked the Tories for years. It hadn't only lost them a natural consistency amongst the gay community, but had also become a key part of the Tories' image as a nasty, backward looking bunch. He had no desire to be involved with the erosion of freedom, but was weighing it up against the possibility that he might be able to do more good from within the government than outside it.

James considered these issues while striding towards Kingsway. The air was still hot and a number of people were out and about, seemingly in no hurry to get home. It wasn't that government ministers were incapable of walking and thinking at the same time but he was feeling tired, so entered Red Lion Square to sit and think things over more clearly. Whilst considering his position in the government, however, now he was also forced to contemplate his position in the square. He recalled briefings about public spaces at night, though the whips' list of verboten places did not include Red Lion Square. They had managed to issue a warning about the obvious Heaths and Commons.

He decided he was safe. And after all, Red Lion was arguably London's most political square, after Trafalgar, of course. Before it existed in its current form, this was the place that a vengeful Charles II had brought the corpses of leading Parliamentarians prior to their trial and 'execution'. Nearly three hundred years later, in 1974, the square had been the scene of a violent clash between left-wing groups and the National Front. That had centred on Conway Hall in the square's far corner; the South Place Ethical Society's meeting hall was named in honour of anti-slavery campaigner Moncure Conway. The socialist writer and painter William Morris had lived at number 17. More amusingly and less overtly political, another resident was the painter Rossetti, whose landlord had warned the artist to keep his models decently attired.

Recalling these facts, James settled back in his seat and pulled a bottle of water from his bag. What a bloody week, he thought, and more to come. More revelations, leaks, policies, initiatives and inexact denials and/or confirmations.

He wasn't sure at what point he believed himself to be talking out loud, but it was quite quickly that he realised that, above the drone of the city, other voices seemed to be outlining the thread of his own thoughts.

The first voice, it soon became clear to James, belonged to someone by the name of Henry Ireton, a former soldier.

'I see the government's in trouble again. Divided between themselves. The Leveller tendency has woken up but it's their own entire fault, too little conciliation, too many arrogant displays of power. They could have sorted it all out earlier with a little judicious compromise, don't you think?'

Another voice, belonging to a mister John Bradshaw, answered.

'I believe they have a different word for Levellers these days. For my own part, I cannot help feeling quite pleased at the news, for I feel the government course much mistaken. What do they expect, sir? Playing with the very fabric of British society? The rights we fought for: to walk the streets beholden to no king or other authority figure unless a properly constituted law has been broken. Furthermore, they go some way to restricting the freedom to criticise religion.'

Here, a third man interrupted him.

'Not all bad considering the blasphemies I see about me today!'

Straining his eyes to see to the other side of the park, James made out the three figures who seemed to be engaged in a passionate and very well informed political debate.

The first speaker was talking again, addressing the third. 'Well you would say that, Oliver. But where shall it lead? A return to superstition, I say. Where anything that flies the flag of a godhead – however ridiculous – is safe from even the faintest trace of mockery. Why, then, where are we?'

'Sir,' answered Oliver. 'Without standards of some sort, where would we be? Worse than the Mohammedans, I'd say!'

Bradshaw laughed. 'That is precisely the sort of comment that could cause a man to be arrested. Did we not fight for freedom?'

'We fought for freedom from tyranny and for a man to worship as he pleased,' rejoined Oliver, 'but not for any spurious right in general. Weeds and nettles, briars and thorns, have thriven under the shadow of freedom, disentitlement and division, discontentment and dissatisfaction. These measures, which you refer to as restrictions, I call necessary steps by a firm government in the face of a real threat. I would suggest you look to Ireland for an analogy.'

Ireton turned to him, saying, 'I might turn that very reminder on you sir! A wound barely healed to this day. Furthermore, think of your own words on overweening government. That the creation of a pretended fear lest error should step in, is like the man that would keep all the wine out of the country lest men should be drunk. It will be found an unjust and unwise jealousy, to deny a man the liberty he hath by nature upon a supposition that he may abuse it.'

'Ah, Henry! You would always use what weapons were to hand best but this government is taking up the righteous judgement of God upon these barbarous wretches, who have imbrued their hands in so much innocent blood.'

James, who had studied master orators and written enough speeches of his own and for others, was struck by the clarity and power of the men's language, even if it was a tad archaic. Nevertheless, he had got out his notebook, because they were using some beautiful, expressions, and he didn't want to forget them, including this line from Bradshaw:

'Here it is my turn to quote your own words Oliver. Necessity has no law. Feigned necessities, imagined crises are the greatest cozenage that men can put upon the Providence of God, and make pretences to break known rules by.'

Oliver responded quickly. James got the impression that he would have liked to sound light-hearted but was constitutionally unable to manage it. He was also beginning to get the idea that this wasn't the first time these three had held this particular debate.

'But sirs, these fanatics who claim, as we did, to be instruments of God, have no truck with Parliament. We studied the glory of God, and the honour and liberty of Parliament together, that is what we fought for. I profess I could never satisfy myself on the justness of war, but from the authority of the Parliament to maintain itself in its rights; and in that cause was an honest man and single-hearted.'

Bradshaw cut in. 'But here, when Parliament itself threatens honest men? And do not, in their defence, these latest fanatics claim that a few honest men are better than numbers?'

'They usurp the term, for when we were soldiers we did not cease to be citizens above others, we did not murder indiscriminately. We cut off a man's head but that man's head had a crown on it and that man was fairly tried a tyrant,' Oliver replied tartly.

'Just so,' nodded Bradshaw, 'but again I implore you to consider your own council that sometimes it is necessary to do not what the public want but what is good for them. As to cutting heads? What better example for not trusting the mob's cheering and baying, for they might shout as much if you or I were going to be hanged.'

'Well, yes,' said Oliver ruefully, rubbing his neck. 'What worries me more is not these specific measures against an identified threat but that a government should make its rule perpetual. In every government there must be something fundamental, somewhat like a Magna Carta, that should be standing and unalterable but I fear power concentrating now to the detriment of all England.'

Ireton sighed. 'So we are in agreement, really, and you just wished a verbal joust!' With that he snatched a paper from a nearby bin.

James watched as the three figures drifted apart and vanished rather abruptly. He stood up and strode across the park towards where the voices had been, but no one was to be seen. He glanced up and down but, aside from a fox imperiously stalking around the rubbish bin, there was nothing. Shrugging his shoulders, he picked up his bag and walked towards Holborn Station, which was by now closed. He hailed a taxi, inside which he began to compose his resignation speech.

Had James (by now the backbench member for Birmingham Sutton Coldfield) returned the following night, he would have found the figures once more glancing through discarded papers, this time screaming of resignations and rebellion by key sections of the government.

Ireton was quoting one of the resignation speeches before adding to his friend, 'sound familiar, Oliver?'

'It does, somewhat. Fine words. A government employee?'

Ireton glanced at Oliver. 'They are your words, slightly paraphrased! He continues in the same furrow but saying that necessity has no law and that that staged crises and imagined necessities by a government are a crime against the people

Oliver spluttered. 'But these are my words! What coxcomb quotes me now? Hand me the paper!'

Ireton passed it over and, after a moment or two, Oliver said, 'This fellow, I recognise him. Under-secretary, is he?'

Bradshaw glanced up from his own inspection of a celebrity libel trial and said, 'He was, yes, but you may know him from somewhere else. He was sitting on the bench over there just last night.'

'Like a common drinker? I wonder how much notice anyone will take of such a man. As we all know, it is good that the State, in choosing men to serve it, takes no notice of their opinions.'

'Yet you served it with opinions aplenty!' said Ireton to Bradshaw, laughing, which appeared to incense the third man.

'Bah! You two are no company for a man whose mind wishes to be engaged by serious matters!'

And with that, the former Lord High Protector of England vanished and Bradshaw returned to reading about the celebrity libel trial, while Ireton checked out the sports pages.

BACK AT ECHO

SHANE WAS STILL SHAKING HIS HEAD AT SOPHIE.

'That was far and away the worst gag I've heard all night and believe me, I've heard some terrible ones already.'

'Oh dear. How was your evening?' Sophie played with her silver pendant as she rolled her eyes at Pearl.

'It was mostly spent walking around viewing London with about twenty former colonials and a very vexing northerner who had no ration on chat.' Shane paused. 'I guess if you've never been to London it might have been OK but I was bored silly by most of it.'

'So you won't be recommending it to your readers?' Pearl asked.

'No I don't think so. I've got the article composed in my head if I can still remember it tomorrow.'

'They do get everywhere, don't they darling? I was at Tenter Ground last Friday evening and there were three groups of them, all two-score strong, within a few yards of each other. Silly. One hopes those Ripper ones start with the line, 'Remember women have died to make this entertainment possible.' Sophie looked directly at Shane and asked, 'So you didn't meet anyone nice to talk to?'

'Well, no. But I did meet someone afterwards as I was heading away from the pub.' Shane was drunk enough to raise the subject, but sober enough not to tell everything. 'A strange woman gave me this.' He handed the ribbon to Pearl. 'Odd looking girl. It occurred to me that this is something your mate Emma Louise might be interested in? Could I call her about it, perhaps?'

Pearl turned the ribbon over and looked at the name and numbers written on it before handing it on to Dean. She fished for her phone to get Emma Louise's number, as Shane carried on talking.

'I didn't think too much of it, but then when I was walking towards the bus-stop I saw a whole load of these ribbons tied to a gate on Redcross Way.'

'Oh, I know where you mean!' cried Sophie. 'It's near Borough Market, isn't it? Someone puts these all over the gate. I'll tell you who knows about that, Pearl's mate Mr London. I remember him telling me about it.'

Shane spoke again. 'Oh yes, I wanted to talk to him anyway, I need to ask him about people objecting to the walking tours in Spitalfields. He lives there, doesn't he? Older geezer, a technician at Chelsea College, right?'

Pearl seemed confused, so Shane prompted her further. 'You know, he used to be mates with that character Martin someone.'

Dean seemed to have woken up. 'Martin? Chelsea Martin? Got some great stories about him, I did a project with him once. He had me filming this Australian guy he'd convinced into believing he could time-travel.'

Finally Pearl realised who they meant. 'Ah, Mr London! You mean Carl, don't you? No, he never lived in Spitalfields, he's always lived in Lambeth.'

'Carl! Yeah that's him. Always full of London tales, really knows his stuff. Do you still see him?'

Pearl thought about it and said, 'Do you know, I haven't for a while. I'm not sure he'd be much use anyway. The last time I saw him he told me he'd stopped pondering London's mysteries. Said it had become too much and he was boring himself.'

'Yeah, he was a bit recherché,' laughed Dean. 'He used to devote hours to topics like how do the people who used to beg for used travel cards make money now. What became of the Peruvian nose flutists on the South Bank. Vital stuff like that.'

'So he just stopped studying the city, just like that?'

'Seems so! Of course he could have had a relapse,' said Pearl.

'No need, no need for Mr London. I know the answer!' interjected Sophie. 'The ribbons are on the gate of the old prostitute cemetery. There's some campaign to make it into a park with a statue and what have you, but it's cemented over just now. The names on them are of the dead toms and the numbers are their dates of birth and death. See here – your ribbon says 1678 08 06 1703. This Alice Street of yours died when she was twenty-five, Shane.' She turned to him and asked, 'Where did you say you got it?'

Shane was silent, comprehension slowly dawning on him, flicking into life like a low energy light bulb. 'Excuse me,' he said, 'I think I need the loo.'

Sophie watched his retreating figure and said. 'Well, that was odd. But not quite as peculiar as Carl giving up on London. Cheers!'

CARL: THE MODERN JOHNSON

I t was one of those winter days in London Town when the greyness and rain make the fissures between one century and another open and the time zones blur. The 19th, 20th or 21st century – in murk like this, it could be any of them. I was feeling out of time, or rather, out of sorts myself as I slouched along the bleak streets past the old Horsemonger Gaol, and headed north towards the funnel of the bridge, gannet mac wrapped tight and bowler fiercely clamped down. Something was not right. I was feeling decidedly peculiar, and that cough I seemed to have picked up surely belonged to someone else. I slipped into the chemist near the police station in search of relief.

There was a small, sniffling queue inside, made up mostly of pensioners. The shop itself had an elderly feel to it as well. There were boards displaying tinctures in one of the windows and, while not exactly dingy, it lacked the astringent brightness of the modern apothecary. My fellow customers were a mixed bunch economically, but I suspected my mother might have delineated them without too much bother. As a locum pharmacist she has a unique take on the British class system and will never describe an area as rich or poor, but instead categorises it by drug. So she might say, 'That's a high codeine linctus prescription area' to denote a run-down neighbourhood. Codeine linctus (known as codex in some parts) is a cough medicine containing traces of opiate, which, taken in sufficient quantities, can result in quite a pleasant junkie nod, and cheaper than the real thing. With the price of illegal drugs falling all the time, you can appreciate that codex abuse is a better social signifier of poverty than Burberry sightings.

Behind the counter was a hunched figure with the best Piccadilly weepers I'd ever seen. He was caped to within an inch of 1878. I could tell this by the cross-weave on his garment, which had only come in that year and ceased to be fashionable on the arrival of the newer India weave in 1882. He clocked my approach, my bowler, my gannex, and raised a quizzical eyebrow. 'Yes?'

'Codex,' I said. 'Codex linct…' (I spluttered) '…for my cough.'

He stared for a while and said, 'Codex, yes. I know what ails you, and codex might be the very thing. It's quite advanced, your condition, isn't it? And the only way to get it out is to get some in!' He emphasised the last words, breaking them up and barking them slightly, as if giving a command. 'Get! Some! In!'

A lost memory flared inside my head. The national service comedy written by John Esmonde that ran from 1975 to 1978 starring Robert Lindsey in his first major TV role, as reformed Teddy boy Jakey Smith. That had been called Get! Some! In!

The shopkeeper leaned over the counter top and whispered excitedly, with a gleam in his eye, 'Yes, we can definitely sort you out, but it's not available over the counter, not what you need. Meet Lily in five minutes by the Marshalsea wall'. He indicated with his chin a whey-faced urchin with dark unruly hair and glittering eyes who looked as if she'd been brought up on a diet of apples and whelks. She slid off the back counter like an eel and, without taking her eyes off me until the last moment, vanished behind a saloon door in a flash of white (it was hard to describe exactly what she was wearing without the words 'bleached hessian sack' coming to mind).

I looked up, blinked and said, 'Eh? How much?'

'Oh we'll come to some arrangement, I'm sure', he said. 'Now, will there be anything else?'

In order to hide my embarrassment from the crowd of pensioners and schoolgirls behind me, I ordered a couple of packets of Protex Blue and some sweet whistles before leaving the shop without a glance over my shoulder. Maybe he did have me down as a drug fiend after all – and what was all that nonsense about the Marshalsea?

The wall was a couple of minutes' away, past St George's – the so-called 'Little Dorrit Church' – in what was Dickens Central. The Marshalsea was a prison for debtors, including Charles Dickens' father for a brief spell. It was grim place that belonged to an era when large sections of Borough formed a criminal slum, not somewhere safe for Foxton minis. Bit of a cheek for him to assume I'd know where the exact place was, though.

To get to the only extant bit of wall, it's a question of moving down an alley, which jerks off to the right alongside the Harvard library. This incorporates the splendid Southwark local history archives. Unable to resist popping in, and knowing that I had a few minutes to kill, I passed through its 1970s corporation portals and opened one of the press cuttings filing cabinets at random. I have often found that a strange serendipity sometimes works when I do this, revealing answers to questions that I hadn't thought of asking yet. The drawer I selected now was full of information about trees and their demise, so by the time I emerged from the library I had been enriched with the knowledge that the London plane tree thrives in the city because of its ability to shed not only its leaves but also its bark, thereby allowing it to rid itself of any build-up of toxins it might pick up by living on London's streets. There was also a bit about Black Sally's Tree in Hyde Park, an elm tree haunted by Sally, who had been murdered as she slept underneath its canopy.

Black Sally wasn't standing outside the library, but Lily was waiting for me by the wall, wearing a sort of woollen ensemble over her rough smock. What was most arresting about her, apart from the glittering eyes, were her shoes, which were at once stylish and clumpy, a confection of buckles and a Westwood of surfaces. She sidled forward and handed me a padded envelope.

'It's all in there. Instructions and everyfing, 'e told me not to charge you nuffink but said 'e would count it a definite favour if you never come back to the shop.'

'Did he say why?' I enquired, puzzled.

'No, and I didn't think to ask, but best do as he says, eh?' She gave me another look and held her glance for just that extra fraction, in which comfortable crosses over into its opposite. 'It's all there, 'e said you'd understand. I'd best be off, I'm a working girl, after all.' She smiled knowingly at the double entendre and slipped through the hole in the wall that lead to the former cemetery of St George's. I stood watching her slight figure diminish, before heading back towards the library with my envelope.

This time I entered the main library next door, which is both more comfortable and less crowded. Selecting a seat near the video collection, I carefully opened the envelope and found it to contain a sheet of paper and a floppy disk. The paper was faded and not of the best quality, and the writing was an odd sort of purple. It took me a minute to recognise it as a mimeographed sheet, of the kind formerly used for duplicate notes at school. It was always rumoured that sniffing a fresh batch would give off a brief high. This one had no odour and its text was composed of a variety of fonts and styles, like an old playbill or advert for quack cures.

☞ DO YOU FIND YOURSELF INDULGING IN RANDOM BOUTS OF FACT-SPIELING ABOUT OBSCURE STREETS IN EC1? ☞ DO YOU HAVE

AN UNNATURAL FASCINATION FOR LONG EXTINCT **ROUTEMASTER** BUS ROUTES? ☞ DO YOU FIND YOURSELF RUMINATING ON JUST WHY THE TOPS OF STATIONS ON THE **NORTHERN LINE** ARE DOMED? ☞ DO YOU HAVE AN UNHEALTHY INTEREST IN FORMER CEMETERIES OR LOST WATERWAYS? ☞ DO YOU COMPETITIVELY QUOTE OBSCURE **IAN DURY** LYRICS?

IF YOU ANSWERED 'YES' TO MORE THAN ONE OF THE ABOVE QUESTIONS, YOU COULD BE SUFFERING FROM **LONDON ELMS DISEASE (LED)**. THIS MALADY STRIKES BOTH GENDERS, ALL AGES AND ALL RACES, BUT IS MOST **PREVALENT AMONGST MALES** BETWEEN THE AGES OF TWENTY-FIVE AND FIFTY. IN ITS EARLY STAGES IT CAN SEEM QUITE A BENIGN AFFLICTION, ENCOURAGED BY FRIENDS WHO ARE HAPPY THAT AT LAST YOU HAVE A HOBBY. BUT IT CAN TAKE HOLD SWIFTLY AND, BEFORE YOU KNOW IT, YOU ARE UNABLE TO HOLD NORMAL CONVERSATIONS AND FIND YOURSELF RAMBLING INCOHERENTLY AT JOB INTERVIEWS ABOUT ELEPHANTS BURIED AT THE HANGER LANE GYRATORY OR **TREES DONATED BY HITLER** TO A NORTH LONDON COLLEGE. PERHAPS YOU HAVE FOUND YOURSELF WANDERING AIMLESSLY, TRYING TO CROSS OFF ALL THE STREETS IN **THE A-Z** OR TAKING DANGEROUS **CROSS-LONDON HIKES** FOR NO OTHER PURPOSE THAN TO fiND A RUMOURED WAR MEMORIAL TO **FIGHTING ANIMALS IN KILBURN**. IN THE ADVANCED STAGES OF LED, THE SUFFERER STARTS TO SHUN NORMAL SOCIETY AND SEEKS OUT FELLOW VICTIMS IN OBSCURE WEBSITE FORUMS, DUSTY ARCHIVES OR **DIMLY LIT BOOZERS** WITH GOOD GHOST STORIES ATTACHED TO THEM AND AN INTERESTING PUB SIGN. THERE, THE SHUT-IN WILL PUT UP WITH ANY AMOUNT OF ARCANE NONSENSE ABOUT **METROPOLITAN CATTLE WATER TROUGHS** IN ORDER TO DELIVER THEIR OWN MONOLOGUE ON THE FATE OF THE **WELSH CHEESEMAKERS** WHO MIGRATED TO LONDON IN THE 1850S. IF THIS HAS HAPPENED TO YOU OR SOMEONE CLOSE: **DO NOT FEAR! HELP IS AT HAND!** THERE IS A CURE, BUT IT IS NOT EASY; NOR IS IT TO BE TAKEN LIGHTLY. FOR THE ONLY WAY TO STOP THIS CURSE IS TO PASS YOUR MISFORTUNE ON TO SOMEONE ELSE. IF YOU ARE CERTAIN THAT YOU WANT TO PROCEED, TURN TO THE NEXT PAGE.

I paused to wipe moisture from my face. I was sweating cobs and, I realised from the strange looks I was receiving from some of the people near me, must have been reading part of the document out loud, or at least with my lips moving. I was stunned. This is clearly what my problem was. It wasn't the London ague (a water-borne complaint that Charles I and Oliver Cromwell suffered from) or a particular-based lung disorder. I had LED. Sheepishly glancing around me, I wondered if anyone could tell just by looking at me. Was my behaviour odd in any way? Were there other sufferers or ex-sufferers present who recognised the document? I shielded the paper from sight and glanced furtively about me before proceeding.

To my left, a gentleman in a deerstalker shuffled in his seat, while a retired footballer returned to the sports pages. I turned to the next page. At the top was a warning.

IF YOU HAVE REACHED THIS POINT, THEN IT IS SAFE TO ASSUME THAT YOU — OR A LOVED ONE — ARE INDEED IN THE GRIP OF **LED**, SO READ ON CAREFULLY.

LED IS A SOCIAL DISEASE PASSED BY VARIOUS MEDIA. YOU CAN CATCH IT FROM PAPER, CONVERSATION AND EVEN THE RADIO. ALTHOUGH NOT EVERYONE IS SUSCEPTIBLE, IT IS NOT KNOWN WHETHER THERE IS A GENETIC OR OTHER COMPONENT. AT ONE TIME, **LED** WAS THOUGHT TO BE QUARANTINED WITHIN THE ORBITAL MOTORWAY BUT CASES HAVE RECENTLY BEEN DISCOVERED AS FAR AFIELD AS **NEWCASTLE** AND EVEN **CANADA**. THE FORMER OUTBREAK WAS TRACED TO A VISITING GEORDIE FOOTBALL FAN WHO GOT LOST IN THE **ELEPHANT AND CASTLE** UNDERPASSES AFTER AN AWAY GAME AT **CHARLTON**. IN THIS EXAMPLE, SYMPTOMS INCLUDED A GROWING FONDNESS FOR WATERCRESS AND **CHAS AND DAVE**, AND A DRAMATIC SWITCHING OF ALLEGIANCE TO BRENTFORD. THE CANADIAN CASE WAS EVEN MORE TRAGIC, THE INUIT VICTIM FREEZING TO DEATH AFTER INSISTING ON WEARING ONLY A CAPE AND BOWLER IN THE **ARCTIC WASTES** AND REFUSING HIS TRADITIONAL DIET OF SEAL IN FAVOUR OF EELS, WHICH ARE COMPARATIVELY RARE IN **NUNAVUT**. HIS MOCK **GEORGIAN IGLOO** HAS SINCE BEEN SENT FOR STUDY TO THE **CENTRE FOR UNCOMMON DISEASES IN TORONTO**.

AS HAS BEEN MENTIONED, THERE IS NO WAY TO CURE EVERYONE; THE ONLY WAY TO GET OUT IS TO GET SOMEONE ELSE IN. THE DISK YOU SHOULD HAVE RECEIVED WITH THIS DOCUMENT HOLDS THE KEY. THINK CAREFULLY BEFORE YOU USE IT!

YOUR CURE (AND THE PLAGUE ON OTHERS)

THIS DISK CONTAINS THE **LONDON GENERATOR.** ☞ CLICK THE BUTTON TO RELEASE HAPHAZARD COLLECTIONS OF LONDON TRIVIA. ☞ WHILE DOING SO, YOU MUST CHANT: 'I NO LONGER CARE WHY WALWORTH IS SO NAMED, NOR WHY THOMAS CUBITT SHOULD BE FAMED, OR THAT PRINCE MONOLULU ONCE DRANK IN THAT BAR, OR DIANA DORS SAVED ALBERT BRIDGE IN HER CAR!'

☞ FOR MOST EFFECTIVE RESULTS, SEED AS MANY **COMPUTERS** AS POSSIBLE WITH THE PROGRAMME CONTAINED ON THE DISK; BETTER YET, INCLUDING THE PROGRAMME ON A WEBSITE WILL ENSURE A WIDER SPREAD. ☞ HAVING DONE SO, YOU MUST THEN PROCEED TO **THE THAMES** AT LOW TIDE AND BURY BOTH THE DISK AND THIS DOCUMENT.

FOLLOW THESE INSTRUCTIONS TRUE THEN **LED** WILL DEPART FROM YOU!

AS SOON AS ONE OTHER PERSON DEVELOPS **LED**, YOU WILL NOTICE YOUR OWN SYMPTOMS DIMINISHING, YOUR WARDROBE AND CONVERSATION RETURNING TO NORMAL AND GREATER **SOCIAL ACCEPTANCE** OUTSIDE THE M25 ORBITAL AREA.

There was no signature, no statement of responsibility; only the Post Office box number 0333300246, London NE1.

That was clearly no use, I thought. Everyone knows there's no NE postal region in London. 'NE' means Newcastle, not North East London, just as 'S' means Sheffield, not South London. I pondered over this possible clue – that might refer to the northern sufferer. Had a Geordie really found the only way of cracking LED? Then I realised the number was far too big to be a PO box number. I found out later that it was, as I had suspected, the International Standard Book Number of The London Encyclopeadia 1983 edition.

I abandoned my trip to St Magnus the Martyr, where I had been going to look at the wooden representation of Old London Bridge, and struck out for home. Once there and settled, my thoughts turned to the disk. This was clearly a joke, a spoof. LED, indeed! The very idea of a London fixation as a communicable disease! Then a cold shudder ran through me as I considered the matter further. What chimed particularly unpleasantly was my own harsh dismissal of the PO box number... 'everyone knows there's no NE postal region in London. 'NE' means Newcastle...' But not everyone knew that. Not everyone would even bother to care to know. It was just the sort of arcane trivia that only someone sickening with the LED would spot immediately. I glanced up at my bookshelves and across to my wardrobe with mounting terror. 'Oh no! Oh God, oh Jesus Christ, no!' I exclaimed in a rough impersonation of Edward Woodward in the Wicker Man. But it wasn't a flaming death accompanied by Christopher Lee and Britt Ekland leading villagers in a folk song that awaited me. No – worse than that, it was the living hell of a London obsessive doomed forever to walk the avenues and alleyways, perpetually searching for that elusive singing milkman of old Hatcham or the legendary boozer in Maida Vale where David Bowie and Marc Bolan agreed that one would be leader of glam rock before handing over to the other. I saw my future as a series of abortive trips to long-bulldozed buildings and covered canals and, with a yell that tore the skies above my home in Conrad Row, I screamed, 'NOOOOOOOOOOOOO!'

There was clearly only one thing to do. With a shaking hand, I placed the disk in my computer and opened the file, chanting self-consciously as I did so. It did exactly what it said it would, and produced a random jumble of London facts and trivia. They formed irregular patterns that still, in a peculiar fashion, formed an intelligent composition. Like London itself (I thought for the last time), they created chaotic idiosyncratic structures that developed in strange and unpredictable ways.

I uploaded the file to my website and, with a bit of tinkering, I had a working model up there. How long would it take to work? I rapidly logged onto a number of web forums, more than I can now remember – Urban 75 was certainly one – and laid a trail to my own website. Surely someone would follow it, someone would be drawn in. In a daze, I hastened to the Thames, where I thrust the disc into the mud, and hurried home. Feverously, I mixed myself a whisky and milk before retiring to my bed.

I must have dozed right off. My sleep was punctuated by dreams about necropolis railways, draymen chasing Austrians and abolishionist churches in Clapham but when I woke I felt much calmer and, by the time I'd finished my breakfast, I felt, as if something had been lifted from me. The interweb never sleeps; and nor do its denizens. Maybe some insomniac cockney or curious ex-pat had found the link. I barely cared, and quickly expunged any guilt with a swift rendition of 'The only way to get some out is Get! Some! In!', which I found strangely hard to recall.

It was some weeks before I ventured down Borough High Street again and, despite the admonishment not to, I couldn't resist going into the apothecary's one last time. It was lighter than I remembered it and more modern. It was Lily I saw first but I barely recognised her; she was wearing a pink T-shirt emblazoned with the slogan 'Total Hottie', a Diesel denim skirt and trainers, and her hair was carefully coifed into a bob. But there was no mistaking the eyes, shiny, dark, but less fierce, with a hint of amused detachment in her features and less of her previous intensity. The shopkeeper stood to her left wearing a lightweight suit.

'Well, sir,' He said. 'Well, well, well. I'd hardly have known you! Not feeling so particular now?' He burst out laughing, Lily joined in and, much to the bemusement of the queue behind me, so did I.

NOTES ON THE STORIES

The Southwark (or Winchester, after the Bishop of Winchester) Geese were a feature of South Bank life for centuries until the Commonwealth (1649-1660). Oliver Cromwell had the theatres closed, the brothels shut, the maypoles chopped down and made all manner of other mischief. These actions made him unpopular on the southside of the Thames but were not the reason Charles II lost no time bringing him (and Ireton and Bradshaw) to trial after the Restoration of the monarchy. Their being dead did not deter Charles, who had them dug up, tried, hung, drawn and quartered. Prior to this indignity the bodies were laid together in (what is now) Red Lion Square and their ghosts are said to haunt that spot. Much of that story's dialogue consists of quotes from Cromwell himself.

If you think that's strange, try visiting the Dolphin Pub with its haunted clock at the corner of the Square. Pubs, perhaps surprisingly, are not the most haunted buildings in London. That distinction goes to the theatre and its successor, the cinema. Notting Hill Coronet Cinema has been both and is regularly visited by the shade of a cashier who committed suicide on the premises. The ghostly imprints of the brothers' duel have become increasingly obscure over the centuries as more and more of Bloomsbury has been built over. Allhough in the tradition of new legends for old the appearance of Emma Louise has perhaps balanced the supernatural score in that quarter. Finally, there is that warning about gift horses and mouths. In particular it is very ill advised to ride on the Each Uisge or waterhorse of Scottish legend that devours people, leaving the liver behind. We can only speculate that, being tee-total, the waterhorse became accustomed to rejecting the average Scot's liver on account of the whisky content as, despite the old joke, not many horses walk into bars.

So what happens next? Carl, having shaken off the fearful LED and fled the metropolis, can be found in the satellite coastal towns of the South East. However, you can take the man out of London but can you take London out of the man, or indeed the weirdness surrounding him? Of course you can't, so expect tales of bizarre revenge, the dog-slaughtering Queen of Hearts Cult and solid reasons for avoiding the meat course. Then there is the exposure of penal colonies in East Anglia and events that will amaze at Walton on the Naze, where everything ends and all stories are linked on a spit of land by a lonely beach.